Map of the Ancient World

PHOENICIA

SEA

EGYPT

There's a Monster in the Alphabet
James Rumford

Houghton Mifflin Company

Boston 2002

www.houghtonmifflinbooks.com

The text of this book is set in Cronos.

The illustrations, done in ink, watercolor, and gouache on Arches
paper, were inspired by the Greek artist Psiax, who brought to life the
amazing red and black figures he painted on vases 2,500 years ago.

Calligraphy by the author.

Library of Congress Cataloging-in-Publication Data

Rumford, James.
There's a monster in the alphabet / James Rumford.
p. cm.
Summary: An alphabet book which relates the legend
of Cadmus, the Phoenician hero who brought the alphabet
to Greece and slew a dragon there.
ISBN 0-618-22140-9
1. Cadmus (Greek mythology)—Juvenile literature. [1. Cadmus
(Greek mythology). 2. Mythology, Greek. 3. Alphabet.] I. Title:
There's a monster in the alphabet. II. Title.
BL820.C13 R85 2002
398.2'0938'02—dc21
[[E]]
2001039893

Printed in Singapore
TWP 10 9 8 7 6 5 4 3 2 1

When the alphabet was new, the ancient ones said that **A** was a picture of an ox, **B** was a house, and **C** had the curves of a boomerang.

The ancient ones put the letters together in a special order to tell a story about their hero, whose name was Cadmus.

Cadmus was a handsome young prince from Phoenicia (fun-NEE-sha) who sailed to Greece to seek his fortune.

A was once a
picture of
an ox

When Cadmus arrived in Greece, the gods welcomed him. They gave him a special message: "If you seek your fortune, follow an **ox** with moon-shaped marks. Wherever the ox lies down to rest, there build a city."

As it happened, not far off, Cadmus found an ox with moon-shaped marks. But as soon as the ox saw Cadmus, it took off. Cadmus ran after it. He followed

that ox day and night, over rocky hills, across dry valleys. At last it lay down on a grassy hill beside an old, abandoned **house**.

Looking around, Cadmus exclaimed, "Ox, my friend, you have chosen well! What a wonderful place for a city!"

The ox, of course, said nothing.

C

was once a
drawing of
a boomerang

Hungry after his long journey, Cadmus went into the woods to hunt with his **boomerang**. He brought back game and roasted it over an open fire.

D

was a
picture of
a door

When Cadmus had eaten, he lay back against the ox. After a time he said,
"How will I build a city by myself, ox?"

Again there was no answer. So Cadmus went inside and closed the **door** on the
lonely night.

E
was a person
showing praise

Before Cadmus fell asleep, he praised the gods—for the ox, for the house, and for his good fortune.

Then he added, "And please send me people for my city."

F

was a peg,
a hook,
or a fork

But instead of people, the gods sent a monster to test the young man's courage. The monster coiled itself around the tiny house, hissing and probing with its **forked** tongue. Cadmus awoke with a start.

Z
in the ancient days
followed F
and was a sword

Something—a monster, he thought, an evil spirit perhaps—was outside. He grabbed his **sword** and ran out into the hissing night. But there was nothing. Cadmus called for his ox. No answer.

H

was a fence

When morning came, Cadmus went straight off to look for his ox. As he walked down the hill, the wind hissed in the dry grass. Cadmus laughed to himself and said, "So, it was the wind that woke me up. It wasn't a night monster!"

At the bottom of the hill, Cadmus saw a fence and a small gate.
"How odd," thought Cadmus.

I

was part of
an arm and
a hand

He opened the gate and discovered a beautiful garden and a singing brook.
Enchanted, he knelt and put his **hand** in the cool, clear water.

K

showed
the fingers
and palm
of a hand

He cupped the **palm** of his hand and drank. Suddenly, something knocked him into the water! It was the ox! How glad Cadmus was! "Friend-ox," he said, laughing. "You're alive! Let's go home."

L
was once a
picture of
a goadstick.

But as soon as he tried to goad the ox back up the hill with a long branch, the ox bellowed and took off, knocking him back into the brook.

M

was rippling
water

Then Cadmus heard a hissing noise. It grew louder. The water rose in huge waves.
He turned.

N was the monster

It was the **night monster**!

X

in the ancient days
followed N
and was a fish

But Cadmus wasn't afraid, even though all the **fish** had already leapt out of the water in fear . . .

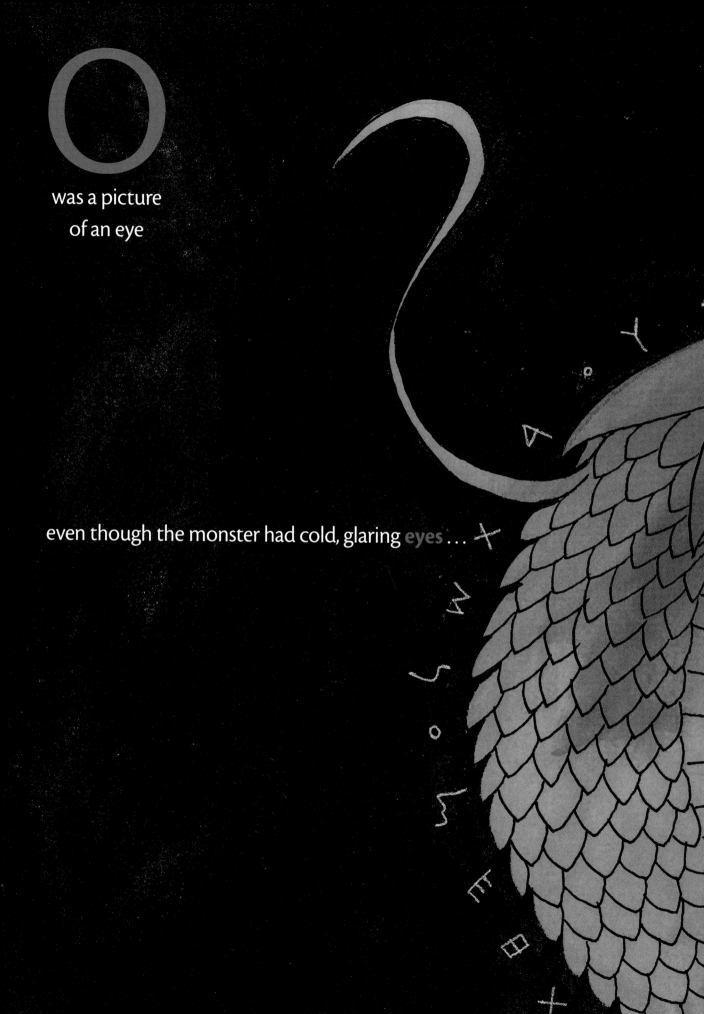

O

was a picture
of an eye

even though the monster had cold, glaring eyes . . .

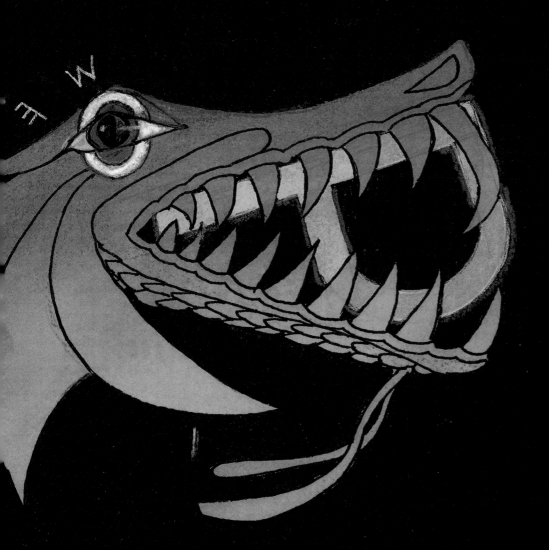

P was a mouth

even though it had a huge, snapping mouth.

Cadmus raised his spear and hurled it. It sank deep into the monster's **neck**.
Down the monster came — with a crash!

may have been
a picture of
a neck

R

was a head

S

was once a
picture of teeth

Suddenly the wind rose in the trees, bringing the voices of the gods.
"Cut off the monster's head!" they roared.
"Pull out the teeth and plant them!" they commanded.

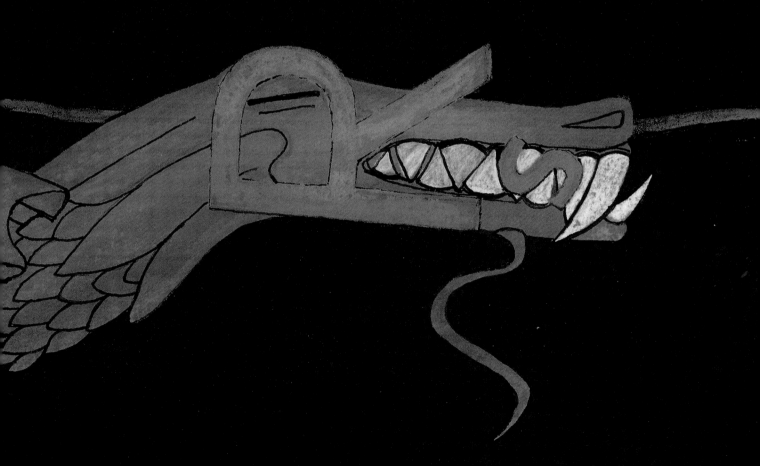

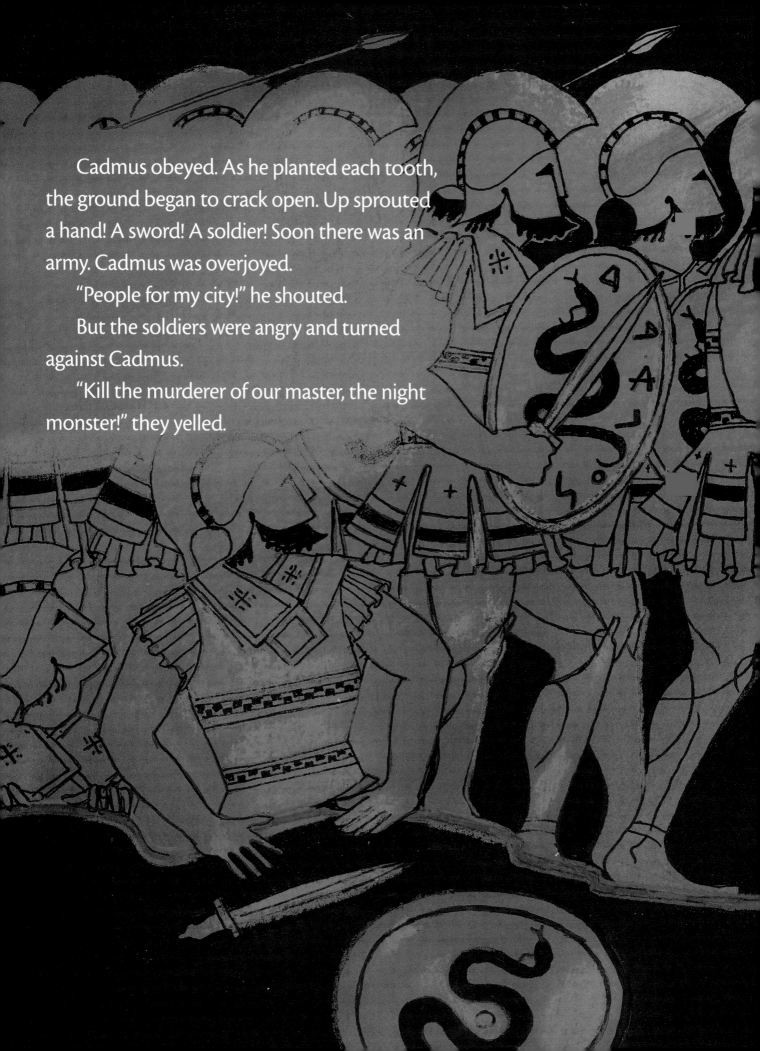

Cadmus obeyed. As he planted each tooth, the ground began to crack open. Up sprouted a hand! A sword! A soldier! Soon there was an army. Cadmus was overjoyed.

"People for my city!" he shouted.

But the soldiers were angry and turned against Cadmus.

"Kill the murderer of our master, the night monster!" they yelled.

Cadmus stepped forward to defend himself.

"Wait!" the gods whispered in Cadmus's ear. "Throw a stone in the air."

Up the stone went. Then down, landing on a soldier, who then accused his neighbor of throwing rocks. There was a push. A shove. Then a brawl. Soldier fought soldier until only five remained. Too tired to fight, the five soldiers knelt before Cadmus.

"Do not kill us!" they pleaded. "We are at your command."

T was once a mark

"Then follow me," said Cadmus.

Cadmus led the men up the hill, where they found the ox waiting.

"Where, ox?" asked Cadmus.

The ox made a mark in the earth with its hoof.

Cadmus's eyes gleamed.

"You brave five," he commanded, "build my city here."

And they did.

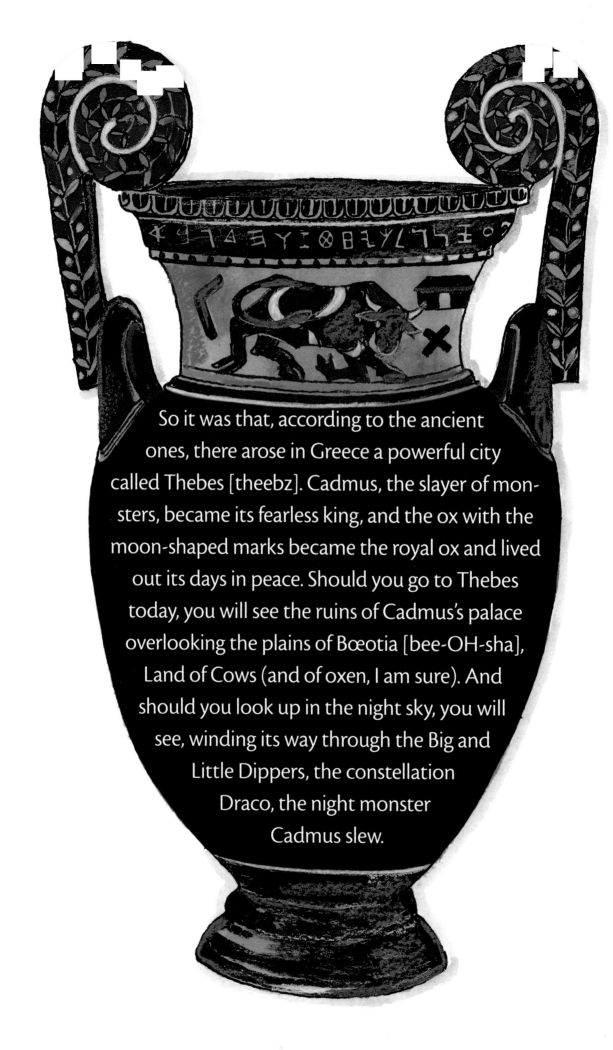

So it was that, according to the ancient ones, there arose in Greece a powerful city called Thebes [theebz]. Cadmus, the slayer of monsters, became its fearless king, and the ox with the moon-shaped marks became the royal ox and lived out its days in peace. Should you go to Thebes today, you will see the ruins of Cadmus's palace overlooking the plains of Bœotia [bee-OH-sha], Land of Cows (and of oxen, I am sure). And should you look up in the night sky, you will see, winding its way through the Big and Little Dippers, the constellation Draco, the night monster Cadmus slew.

According to the ancient historian Herodotus [her-ODD-ih-tuss], Cadmus brought the alphabet to Greece. Cadmus was a Phoenician, and while we do not know if what Herodotus said was true, it is true that the Phoenicians were traders who took their alphabet of twenty-two letters all over the western world.

Very recent discoveries in Egypt have led scientists to believe that our letters were originally pictures. About 3,800 years ago, a Semitic people like those from modern Lebanon or Israel learned from the ancient Egyptians how to make an alphabet by turning pictures into letters. The process was simple. The first sound of the picture was always the sound of the letter. ∿∿∿ was the Egyptian sign for "water." The Semitic word for water began with the sound **m**, so ∿∿∿ became the letter **M**.

The Phoenician alphabet, which appeared about seven hundred years later, also worked the same way. The first sound of the picture became the sound of the letter. A snakelike monster was **nahesh**, so a squiggly picture of **nahesh** became **N**. House was **bet**, so a simple picture of a house became **B**.

Even though we know what the Phoenician names of the letters are, we aren't always sure of their meanings. Some of the meanings have been lost over the last twenty-five centuries. Take **Q**. The Phoenician name was **qof**. Did **qof** mean "neck" or did it mean "monkey"? Some say **Q** shows the monkey's tail; others say the head and neck. These questions will remain until more discoveries are made.

As I studied the ancient alphabet and pondered over what the original pictures must have been, I began to wonder. Did the ancient people put the pictures together in a special order because they wanted to tell a story? Perhaps, but no story has come down to us that fits the ancient pictures . . . except maybe one, the story of Cadmus.

So with a lot of imagination — and help from thick, scholarly books — I retold the myth of Cadmus. I used only the ancient letters still found in our alphabet. I carefully followed the ancient order, putting **Z** after **F** and **X** after **N**. For now, this book is just a story, but maybe, one day, one of you will go digging in the ancient cities and discover why the letters were strung together the way they were.

The Descendants of the Phoenician Alphabet

The Phoenician alphabet is the ancestor of many alphabets. Below are its most famous offspring: English in black, Greek in purple, Hebrew in orange, and Arabic in turquoise. The earliest forms of the letters are in gray and go back before the Phoenician alphabet, to Egypt itself. The link between these forms and Phoenician ones is not certain, and here and there you will see question marks. Don't worry. This just means that there is a lot more for you to discover. We borrowed our alphabet from the Romans who borrowed most of their letters from the Etruscans [ee-TRUSS-kins], who lived in Italy, too. The Etruscans got their letters from the Greeks, who, in turn, got theirs from the Phoenicians. Each time the alphabet changed hands, it was transformed. For example, the Greeks put **Y** at the back of the alphabet along with **X**. The Romans invented **G** and put **Z** at the end. And the Europeans in the Middle Ages invented **J**, **U**, and **W**.

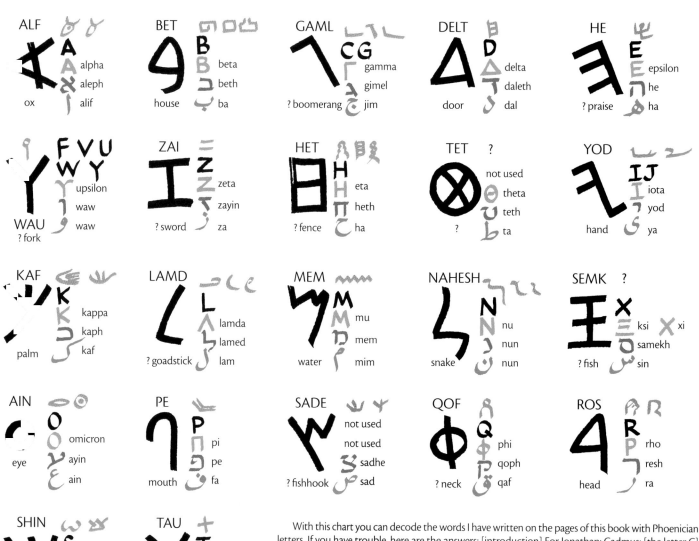

ALF — A, alpha, aleph, ox, alif
BET — B, beta, beth, house, ba
GAML — C, G, gamma, gimel, ? boomerang, jim
DELT — D, delta, daleth, door, dal
HE — E, epsilon, he, ? praise, ha

WAU / ? fork — F, V, U, W, Y, upsilon, waw, waw
ZAI — Z, zeta, zayin, ? sword, za
HET — H, eta, heth, ? fence, ha
TET — ? not used, theta, teth, ?, ta
YOD — I, J, iota, yod, hand, ya

KAF — K, kappa, kaph, kaf, palm
LAMD — L, lamda, lamed, lam, ? goadstick
MEM — M, mu, mem, mim, water
NAHESH — N, nu, nun, nun, snake
SEMK — ? X, ksi, xi, samekh, sin, ? fish

AIN — O, omicron, ayin, ain, eye
PE — P, pi, pe, fa, mouth
SADE — not used, not used, sadhe, sad, ? fishhook
QOF — Q, phi, qoph, qaf, ? neck
ROS — R, rho, resh, ra, head

SHIN — W, S, sigma, shin, shin, ? teeth
TAU — T, tau, taw, ta, mark

With this chart you can decode the words I have written on the pages of this book with Phoenician letters. If you have trouble, here are the answers: [introduction] For Jonathan; Cadmus; [the letter C] The hunter; [the letters I and K] The water of Ares [AIR-eez] (Ares was the god of war and an ancestor of the monster); [the letters O and P] The monster of Ares; [the letter T] The names of the five men were Echion, Oudaeus, Chtonius, Hyperenor, and finally Pelorus [ee-KIGH-on, oh-DAY-us, KTONE-ee-us, high-PURR-en-or, peh-LOR-us]

These three works helped in the writing of this book: Andrew Robinson's *The Story of Writing*, David Diringer's *The Alphabet*, and the book that first got me interested in the history of the alphabet when I was a boy, *The 26 Letters* by Oscar Ogg.

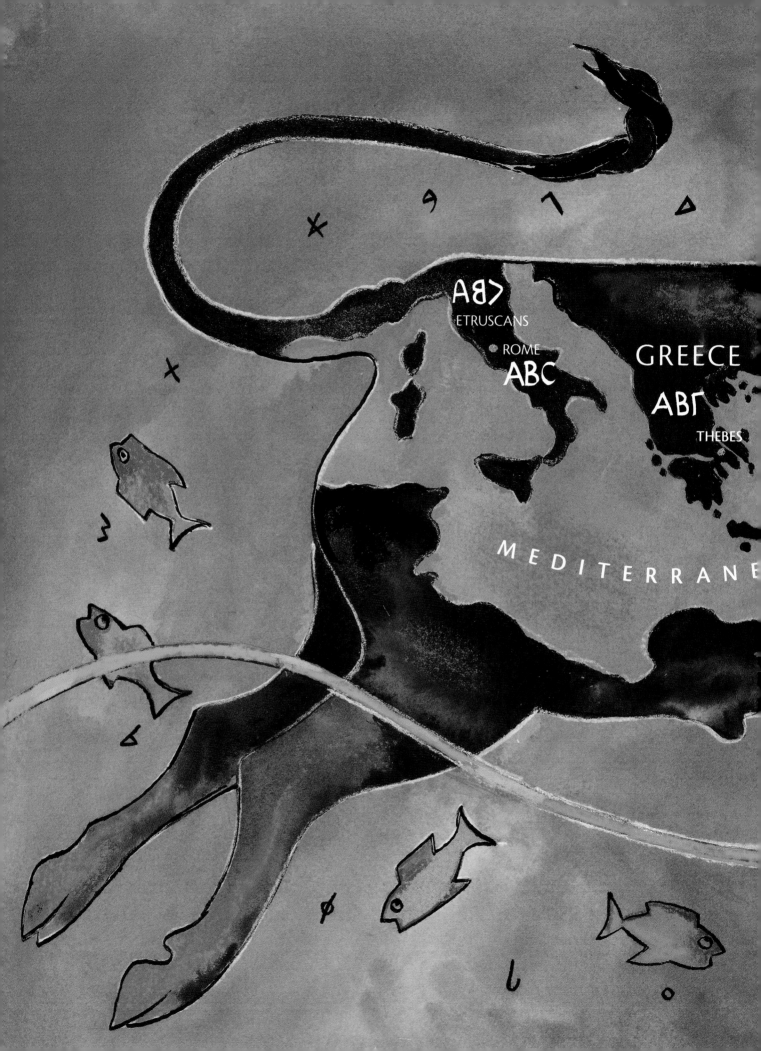